Seaside Lullaby

Text copyright © 2018 by The Creative Company
Illustrations copyright © 2018 by Maria Cristina Pritelli · Edited by Amy Novesky
Designed by Rita Marshall · Published in 2018 by Creative Editions · P.O. Box 227,
Mankato, MN 56002 USA · Creative Editions is an imprint of The Creative Company
www.thecreativecompany.us · All rights reserved. No part of the contents of this book
may be reproduced by any means without the written permission of the publisher.
Printed in China

Library of Congress Cataloging-in-Publication Data

Names: Pritelli, Maria Cristina, illustrator. Title: Seaside lullaby / by Maria Cristina
Pritelli, illustrator. Summary: A sweetly spun lullaby evokes images of the seaside
while describing the cycle of sleep as mimicking the seasons of the year.
Identifiers: LCCN 2017048754 / ISBN 978-1-56846-328-5
Subjects: LCSH: Lullabies. / Seashore—Fiction. / Seasons—Fiction. / Sleep—Fiction.
Classification: LCC PZ8.3.P93653 Se 2018   DDC 782.42 [E]—dc23
First edition 9 8 7 6 5 4 3 2 1

Seaside Lullaby

Maria Cristina Pritelli

Creative Editions

(AUTUMN)

Fall,
falling.

Tousled sheet,
a restless sea.

But then, calm.

Fog tucks in.

And sugar spun
from sea foam...

sweetens the trip
to the deep.

(WINTER)

Night grows...

the dark glows.

Heart beats...

thoughts fleet.

Stars flicker,
from afar.

gather at the shore.

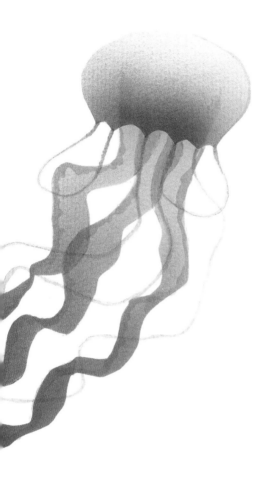

Dream,
dreaming.

A castle, many rooms,
made of sand.

Walking back,

awakening.